The OFFICIAL F·R·I·E·N·D·S

THE TELEVISION SERIES

QUIZ & FILL-IN BOOK!

SCHOLASTIC INC.

All rights reserved. Published by Scholastic Inc., *Publishers since 1920.*
SCHOLASTIC and associated logos are trademarks and/or
registered trademarks of Scholastic Inc.

ISBN 978-1-338-79999-6

10 9 8 7 6 5 4 3 2 1   22 23 24 25 26

Printed in China   62

First printing 2022

Stock photos © Shutterstock.com.

Best friends Rachel, Monica, Phoebe, Joey, Chandler, and Ross are always there for one another, whether it's trying out a new recipe, competing in a sports tournament, hanging out at Central Perk, or lending a helping hand.

When life gets hard, it's the friends who will be there for you that count the most. They'll be there for you for the good times and the bad.

What does friendship mean to you?

Now's your chance to find out! This book is filled with tons of games, writing prompts, and other activities that will show just how good of a friend you really are.

Turn the page to get started!

WHICH *FRIENDS* CHARACTER ARE YOU MOST LIKE?

Moving to the big city can be tough, but with the best group of friends, there's nothing you can't do! It's time to find out for sure whether you're the Phoebe of the gang or a total Chandler. Circle the letter according to your best answer.

1. Your favorite subject in school is:
A. Science
B. Gym class
C. Drama
D. Home economics
E. History
F. Math

2. Your dream job would be:
A. Paleontologist
B. Fashion designer
C. Actor
D. Chef
E. Psychic
F. Writer

3. You won the lottery! The first thing you're spending the money on is:

A. An engagement ring
B. A whole new wardrobe
C. An all-you-can-eat buffet
D. A professional cleaning service
E. A donation to your favorite charity
F. A new house

4. It's the holiday season, and you're spending it with friends. What's your role?

A. Cracking jokes
B. Making dessert
C. Eating everything in sight
D. Setting the table
E. Getting everyone in the holiday spirit
F. Watching the game

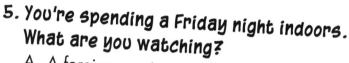

5. You're spending a Friday night indoors. What are you watching?

A. A foreign movie
B. A rom-com movie
C. An action movie
D. A home movie
E. A cartoon
F. A sitcom

6. Your friends would describe you as:

A. Passionate
B. Caring
C. Comic relief
D. A leader
E. Creative
F. Logical

ANSWERS

MOSTLY A's:
ROSS GELLER

You're a total Ross Geller! Just like Ross, you're book smart and are very passionate about what you love. Also, you may like monkeys—but that's just a guess!

MOSTLY B's:
RACHEL GREEN

Just like Rachel, you're confident, smart, and a total fashionista. While you sometimes get wrapped up in your own problems, you are incredibly sweet and fun to be with.

MOSTLY C's:
JOEY TRIBBIANI

How you doin'? Just like Joey, you are good-natured and charming. You have a mean appetite for fun and food and always want to have a good time.

MOSTLY D's:
MONICA GELLER

You're the "Mom"-ica of the group. Between your obsession with cleanliness and your need to boss everyone around, people may think you're a bit high-maintenance. But your real friends always know you always have their back.

MOSTLY E's:
PHOEBE BUFFAY

Just like Phoebe, you tell it like it is. You're earnest, sweet, and a little bit wild. You know that marching to the beat of your own drum (or guitar!) never goes out of style!

MOSTLY F's:
CHANDLER BING

Can you BELIEVE you got Chandler?! You're the sarcastic friend who is always ready with a witty comeback and funny quip. Just don't be afraid to let your guard down in front of your friends!

MONKEYING AROUND!

Ross's white-headed capuchin monkey, Marcel, always creates some mischief within the group. Using the grid, draw your own version of Marcel below! What are some other exotic animals that would be wild to befriend?

....

....

....

Imagine you're a reporter for a BIG New York magazine. Then write an article about one of the six friends below! Has Ross discovered a new dinosaur? Is there a latest fashion don't that Rachel needs to warn us about? It's your article, so you get to choose! When you're done, draw images that match your article.

WOUD YOU RATHER

WOULD YOU RATHER . . .

Grab a good cup of coffee with friends

OR

stay in on a Friday night and order some pizza?

Find a thumb in your soda

OR

lose a fingernail in a quiche?

Eat Mockolate

OR

eat a dessert filled with meat?

Eat spaghetti off the carpet

OR

eat cheesecake off the hallway floor?

Wear stretchy pants to Thanksgiving dinner

OR

put your head in a Thanksgiving turkey?

FOOD EDITION

Be trapped in a room
and forced to eat wax

OR

go to a fancy
restaurant and only
order water?

Eat Ross's
Thanksgiving "Moist
Maker" sandwich

OR

take food from Joey?

Go on a jam-making spree
to get over a breakup

OR

accidentally make
meat lasagna for a
vegetarian?

Drink a gallon of milk
in ten seconds

OR

stick marshmallows
up your nose?

Find out your grandmother's
homemade cookie recipe was store bought

OR

order the
"Joey Special" for one?

A best friend is someone who always has your back and will be there when you need them most—whether that means helping you with a job interview or going for a cup of coffee to talk about life. No matter what,

when it comes to proving what a true friend is, these six friends will always be there for you! But who do you think is the greatest friend and why? Fill out your answers here!

> I think the greatest friend out of the six friends is:

This friend showed they were a good friend when:

....

....

....

Another incredible thing they did was:

....

....

....

Now draw your
character below!

HOW WELL DO YOU KNOW YOUR FRIENDS?

Write down the answers here, and then see how many you got right! But no cheating— Joey doesn't share answers!

1. What is the childhood toy that is nailed to a plank of wood to make the Geller Cup?

2. How many sisters does Joey have?

3. What color are the umbrellas the friends mess around with during the opening credits?

4. What does Chandler tell Janice his address will be in Yemen?

5. What causes the fire in Phoebe's apartment?

6. Which hockey team have the boys gone to watch when Ross gets hit in the face by a puck?

7. Which airport does Rachel's flight to Paris leave from in "The Last One"?

Now design your own dream New York City apartment! Be sure to draw your bed, a cool balcony, and more!

Imagine that you're going to New York City. Of course you won't want to miss Times Square, the Empire State Building, or the Museum of Modern Art (MoMA).

**Where else would you go?
What would you do?
List them below!**

1 ....
2 ....
3 ....
4 ....
5 ....
6 ....
7 ....
8 ....
9 ....
10 ....

Phoebe loves to sing. If you had the chance to write your own song, what would you sing about? Write out the lyrics here—and don't forget to come up with a catchy tune!

Imagine that you get to do anything you'd like for one day in New York City. Check your favorite option for each prompt below.

What's the first thing you do when you wake up?

○ Choose the perfect outfit to wear ○ Fight with my roommate over who gets dibs on the first shower ○ Cook a lavish breakfast ○ Clean up the dishes from the night before ○ Sleep a little bit longer

Who are you eating breakfast with?

○ Monica ○ Ross ○ Chandler ○ Rachel ○ Joey ○ Phoebe

How are you spending your day?

○ Cleaning the apartment

○ Waiting tables ○ Going to auditions ○ Singing in a coffee shop ○ Giving lectures at a college

○ Going to a nine-to-five job

It's Friday night! What are you doing?

○ I have a date! ○ Calling my psychic

○ Ordering in a pizza ○ Taking a stroll around the city

○ Going to a fancy restaurant

Where are you hanging out today?

○ Central Park ○ My regular coffee spot

○ My apartment ○ My BFF's apartment ○ The office

What kind of pet would you take care of for a day?

○ A chicken ○ A duck ○ A monkey

○ A hairless cat ○ A lobster

HOW BIG OF A SUPERFAN ARE YOU?

Have you ever wondered how well you know the TV show *Friends*? Answer the questions below to find out how big of a superfan you are!

1. Which character has a twin?
- A. Rachel
- B. Phoebe
- C. Ross
- D. Monica

2. What nickname did Monica's dad give her?
- A. Tiny Electronica
- B. Small Kazoo
- C. Little Harmonica
- D. Itty-Bitty Trumpet

3. Who is the Manager of Central Perk?
A. Spencer
B. Hunter
C. Jonathan
D. Gunther

4. What is Rachel scared of?
A. Swings
B. Dogs
C. Snakes
D. Heights

5. What word does Ross say he learned in karate?
A. Zanshin
B. Tai chi
C. Unagi
D. Krav Maga

6. Who hates Thanksgiving?
A. Monica
B. Chandler
C. Phoebe
D. Joey

6/6 CORRECT
AWESOME!

There's a Friends expert in the house! If you were competing for Monica's apartment, you'd definitely win!

MORE THAN 3 CORRECT
NICE!

You've definitely seen this show more than once! You didn't remember all the nitty-gritty details but hey, you can always try again.

3 CORRECT
CLOSE!

You're definitely a fan, but you couldn't quite remember all of these details. It's okay, friend!

LESS THAN 3 CORRECT
AW, IT'S OKAY!

You probably love Friends, but it sounds like it's time for another rewatch marathon!

Ross is a paleontologist, aka a scientist who studies fossils like dinosaur bones. While his other friends don't seem very interested, there are so many cool facts we can learn about every day.

What do you know about dinosaurs? Write about your favorite dinosaurs below—and pretend that Professor Geller is doing the grading!

Living in New York will throw a lot of challenges at you. Do you have what it takes? Read each prompt below, and then draw what you'd do in each scenario!

1 NYC pizza is legendary. Draw your go-to order with all your favorite toppings!

2 You're riding the subway, and you give a dollar to a street performer. Draw their performance below!

3 You have a BIG job interview! Draw your impressive interview outfit here!

4 You have a friend visiting from out of town. What NYC landmark are you going to bring them to first? Draw it to the left!

5 B-R-O-A-D-W-A-Y night! What play are you going to see? Draw it here.

Rachel Green is known for her incredible style and her famous haircut. Pretend you are Rachel and it's time for a makeover!

Draw a picture of yourself now on the left and a picture of you after your transformation on the right!

BEFORE

AFTER

Each of the six friends have many personality traits that make them an essential part of the group. Ross is smart. Phoebe is free-spirited. Rachel is kind. Chandler is sarcastic. Joey is goofy. Monica is responsible.

If you were a part of the group, what qualities would you want to have? What personality traits best describe you? Which one of the friends would you want as a best friend?

My qualities are:

....

....

I chose this because:

....

....

....

Out of the six friends, I'm most similar to:

....

I'm most similar to them because:

....

....

....

....

My best friend of the group would be:

....

I would be there for them when:

....

....

....

....

....

Rachel is having a busy day serving up coffee at Central Perk! And all her orders keep coming in wrong . . . through no fault of her own, of course.

Imagine that Rachel is holding the strangest drink combination you can imagine. Draw it in the cup on the next page.

This coffee is made with (check one):

○ Skim milk ○ Oat milk ○ Soy milk ○ Cashew milk
○ Pistachio milk ○ Water

Then mixed with (check one):

○ Rainbow sprinkles ○ Caramel syrup ○ Lukewarm water
○ Green tea ○ Medium roast ○ Hazelnut roast

Then swirled with (check one):

○ Dark roast ○ Kombucha ○ Hibiscus flower
○ Chocolate milk ○ Nacho cheese ○ Beef trifle

Topped with (check one):

○ Strawberries ○ Vanilla foam ○ Guacamole
○ Whipped cream ○ Rainbow food dye ○ A whole donut

It's also got these things (write about all the most interesting ingredients you can add to this drink!):

....

....

....

....

....

I call it: ....

It tastes like: ....

I'd serve this drink to: ....

WOULD YOU RATHER

Have to walk behind a confused tourist family

OR

have to talk to every person with a clipboard on the sidewalk?

Have an infestation of bedbugs

OR

have an infestation of rats?

Get weekly free tickets to a Broadway show

OR

get weekly free tickets to the ice cream museum?

Puke on the train

OR

fall into a garbage pile in the middle of the summer?

NYC EDITION

CENTRAL PERK

Never be able to leave
Times Square

OR

never be able to leave
Central Park?

Have a train pull into
the subway station
any time you want

OR

always be able to find
a cab immediately?

Have your bodega magically stock all
your favorite midnight snacks

OR

have all your BFFs live in
the same neighborhood?

Live in New York City

OR

live anywhere else in
the world?

JOEY DOESN'T SHARE ICE CREAM

Joey likes many foods, but one of his favorites is ice cream. As he says to Ross, "Welcome back to the world. Grab a spoon!"

1. Where is your favorite spot to hang out with your friends?

2. Coffee is the number-one drink in New York City. What's your favorite drink and why?

3. Imagine you were Gunther and opened an ice cream shop called Central Scoop. What top five flavors of ice cream would you serve?

4. What's your favorite flavor of ice cream and why?

5. What toppings would you put on your ice cream?

6. What flavor of ice cream would you NEVER eat? Why?

Which zany guest character on *Friends* are you most like?

1. What's your favorite kind of movie?
A. A comedy
B. A romantic film
C. A foreign film
D. A movie with a scary villain

2. Where can people usually find you?
A. Dancing at the best party
B. Hanging in a coffee shop
C. Working in my office
D. Prank calling my sister

3. What job would you have?
A. Personal shopper
B. Barista
C Agent
D. Waitress

4. What thing sounds the scariest to you?
A. My best friend moving away
B. Unrequited love
C. My coworkers not taking their job seriously
D. Having to admit I was wrong about something

5. What's the thing you're most passionate about?

A. Making people laugh

B. Being myself

C. Working hard

D. Winning

6. If you weren't living in NYC, where would you live?

A. Yemen

B. Paris

C. Los Angeles

D. London

ANSWERS

MOSTLY A's:

JANICE

You're known for your sense of humor, just like Janice. You have an iconic laugh, and everyone knows when you walk in the room.

MOSTLY B's: GUNTHER

You're a romantic, like Gunther. Gunther has a huge crush on Rachel all throughout the show but was no match for her epic romance with Ross.

MOSTLY C's:

ESTELLE

When people think of hard working, they think of you! That's why you're most like Joey's agent Estelle. You're always on the lookout for your friends!

MOSTLY D's: URSULA BUFFAY

You're a troublemaker, like Phoebe's twin, Ursula. You're always causing mischief wherever you go, but deep down we all know you really care!

As we see throughout the show, Rachel is the queen of fashion dos and don'ts. She even becomes a personal shopper for a big department store. Draw two dresses for Rachel to shop for in the space below—and remember, don't be a fashion DON'T!

WOULD YOU RATHER

WOULD YOU RATHER . . .

Be on a soap
opera with Joey

OR

sing a duet with
Phoebe?

Get trapped in
an ATM box with
Chandler

OR

get stuck in
Monica's bedroom?

Travel to China
with Ross

OR

travel to Paris
with Rachel?

Wear a pink Little
Bo-Peep bridesmaid
dress like Rachel

OR

walk around with
an eye patch like
Monica?

FAVORITE FRIEND EDITION

Battle Joey over
a comfy chair
OR
battle Chandler
over a comfy couch?

Have Ross teach you
how to play bagpipes
OR
have Phoebe teach
you to play guitar?

Be Joey's identical
hand twin
OR
be Phoebe's twin?

Do a cheerleading
routine with Rachel
OR
compete with Joey
on a game show?

Chandler is known as the funny guy of the group. He's always making everyone laugh with his one-liners and zingers. Imagine that you are doing a standup routine and use the next few pages to write some of your BEST Chandler-inspired jokes!

When Rachel decides to make a dessert for Thanksgiving, it quickly becomes a disaster! Without realizing that pages of two recipes get stuck together, Rachel accidentally makes one part English trifle and one part shepherd's pie. Luckily for everyone, Joey will eat anything! Use these pages to come up with your own crazy dessert idea!

First, circle as many of the below ingredients as you want.

Avocado	Chocolate chips	Peanut butter
Bananas	Coffee	Soy sauce
Blue cheese	Ketchup	Tofu
Broccoli	Olives	Watermelon
Canned tuna	Onions	Whipped cream

Now write down the instructions for making your dessert! Make sure you include information about how long (and in what direction) to mix things, which order the ingredients need to be added in, and any other important steps.

My dessert is called:

....

My dessert is eaten on this holiday:

....

The first step to making my dessert is:

....

The second step is:

....

The third step is:

....

The fourth step is:

....

The fifth step is:

....

The last step is:

....

You'll know the dessert is ready when:

....

Ross claims to be the master of unagi—a state of total awareness. What is something that you're very skilled at? It could be dancing, cooking, or even karate! Write about it on the lines below.

What makes you a master at this skill?

....

....

....

....

....

How would you teach a friend
who wanted to learn from you?

....

....

....

....

....

What's another skill that you would like to become a master of?

Some kids have two moms, and some kids have two dads. Ross's son, Ben, lives with his two moms, Carol and Susan.

Who do you live with? What is the best part about living with them? Write about it on the lines below, then on the opposite page draw a picture of something fun you do together!

How much do you know about *Friends*? Find out by answering the TRUE/FALSE questions below! You get one point for each right answer.

TRUE/FALSE

1 Ross dresses up as Santa at Christmas for his son, Ben.

TRUE/FALSE

2 Monica's grandmother used to live in Monica's apartment.

TRUE/FALSE

3 Joey got an acting job playing Dr. Drake Ramoray on *General Hospital*.

TRUE/FALSE

4 In the series finale, Chandler and Monica move to Phoenix.

TRUE/FALSE

5 In one episode, Phoebe thought her mom had reincarnated as a cat.

TRUE/FALSE

6 Rachel was supposed to marry Ross in the show's first episode.

TRUE/FALSE

7 Phoebe has an alter ego named Regina Phalange.

TRUE/FALSE

8 If you were going to order the "Joey Special," you'd be ordering one pizza and one sandwich.

TRUE/FALSE

9 Chandler is sent to Tulsa after he falls asleep during a meeting at work.

TRUE/FALSE

10 When the friends are trying to navigate a couch up the stairs, Ross famously yells, "Turn!"

I ♥ FRIENDS

55

9-10 RIGHT ANSWERS

WAY TO GO!

You totally know everything there is to know about *Friends*.

5-8 RIGHT ANSWERS

NOT BAD—

but you might want to do some rewatching.

0-4 RIGHT ANSWERS

IT'S OK—

just watch the show again!

Perhaps nothing is more iconic in the *Friends* universe than the picture frame Monica hangs up over her peephole. In the picture frame below, draw anyone you would want to knock on your door.

Monica and Ross are both fiercely competitive siblings and have been fighting over the Geller Cup since they were young.

If you were competing for a trophy, what would you call it?

....

What would you need to do to win this trophy?

....

....

Now draw yourself receiving the award!

Use these lines to write up an article in the newspaper announcing the award in your honor.

....

....

....

....

....

....

....

WHICH PET WOULD BE BEST FOR YOU?

A lot of fun and silly animals appear in Friends! Answer the questions below to discover exactly which animal would be the best pet for you.

1. Which characteristic best describes your personality?

A. Adventurous
B. Social
C. Withdrawn
D. Loyal

2. How do you feel about your family?

A. They are a good audience.
B. I like them, just as I like my friends.
C. They can sometimes be annoying.
D. They're the most important thing of all.

3. How would you like to be remembered?

    A. A good leader
    B. A best friend
    C. Fashionable
    D. Someone who is always there
       for others

4. You can choose anything you want at a restaurant. What do you pick?

    A. A fruit salad
    B. The vegetarian option
    C. A steak
    D. A fancy dessert

5. What do you like to do when you are at home alone?

    A. Play video games
    B. Go through my siblings' stuff
    C. Curl up with a good book
    D. Call up friends and family
       on the telephone

ANSWERS

MARCEL THE MONKEY

Quit monkeying around! But actually a fun, clever little sidekick would be the perfect pet for you.

MOSTLY B's:

A CHICK AND A DUCK

Why have one pet, when you could have two?! You're all about companionship, so the more the merrier!

MOSTLY C's:

MRS. WHISKERSON THE HAIRLESS CAT

You march to the beat of your own drum and love to be different. A hairless cat says all that and more.

MOSTLY D's:

A LOBSTER

Don't be put off by those claws! Lobsters mate for life, and you're in the market for a best friend till the end.

62

When Chandler gets a new laptop for work, he's so excited about all the specs—of course he much rather use it to play video games! What kind of video game would you want to play? Draw a picture of it on the screen below.

WOULD YOU RATHER

Play dress-up in a wedding dress

play dress-up in a cheerleading uniform?

Be a dessert stealer

be a car thief?

Sing a silly song

do a silly dance to soothe a crying baby?

Go on a string of bad dates

be asked out by someone you don't like?

RACHEL EDITION

Go to a wedding in London

OR

take a dream job in Paris?

Accidentally leave your hair straightener on

OR

break your friend's armchair?

Get a really short haircut

OR

convince your friend to go bald?

Go to prom with your best friend's brother

OR

go with your cousin?

Go for a run with your friend in Central Park

OR

help your friend move a couch?

Monica is known for being an incredible chef. Whether it's a life-changing mac and cheese, a Thanksgiving turkey dinner, or some homemade jam, she's always coming up with something mouthwatering.

Imagine that you are a chef. Create a recipe below! List the ingredients and steps, and draw a picture of your finished product. Don't forget to give your creation a name!

Recipe name:

....

Ingredients:

....

....

....

....

....

Instructions: ....

....

....

....

....

....

....

....

Being a good friend isn't only about hanging out in coffee shops or going shopping together.

What does it mean to you to be a good friend? Use the lines below to write about how you show you're a good friend!

Living MY Best Life WITH FRIENDS

F·R·I·E·N·D·S

WOULD YOU RATHER

WOULD YOU RATHER . . .

Get a spray tan

OR

have extra-shiny white teeth?

Fake a British accent

OR

talk in a secret language?

Snack on some sugary maple candy

OR

snack on a bushel of apples?

Have Monica as your sister

OR

have Joey as your brother?

70

ROSS EDITION

Play a keyboard with only random sounds

OR

play the bagpipes?

Dress up as Spud-nik

OR

dress up as the Holiday Armadillo?

Dig up a T. rex skeleton

OR

dig up a Brontosaurus skeleton?

Although Phoebe is pretty quirky, she's also one of the kindest friends! What's the kindest thing your friends have ever done? Write about it here!

....

....

....

....

....

....

....

....

....

....

....

....

Chandler is never afraid to speak his mind. Think about a time that you believed in something others didn't understand. Then write about it here!

....

....

....

....

....

....

....

....

....

....

....

....

....

Having a sleepover with your best friends can be so much fun! Monica, Rachel, and Phoebe sure know how to bring the fun.

Now imagine that you're at a sleepover with your best friends. What games will you play? What snacks? Write about it below!

Even the greatest friends make mistakes *sometimes*. If you were part of the group, what mistake would you probably make? Answer these questions to find out!

1. What is your best quality?

    A. Sense of humor
    B. Super empathetic
    C. Confidence
    D. Stealth

2. What is your worst quality?

    A. Not knowing when to stop
    B. Jealousy
    C. Your temper
    D. Taking too many risks

3. What sounds like the most fun to you?

A. Tricking a friend into eating wasabi instead of pistachio ice cream
B. Getting through the whole day without losing anything
C. Keeping a list of people who owe you one
D. Sneaking out and sleeping over at your friend's apartment

4. What's your greatest fear?

A. Nobody thinking you're funny
B. Getting your memory erased
C. Not being able to stand up for yourself
D. Being trapped

5. Which *Friends* character would you *least* like to hang out with one-on-one?

A. Chandler
B. Ross
C. Monica
D. Phoebe

ANSWERS

MOSTLY A's: PULLING A PRANK

You're a jokester like Chandler or Joey. And while you love making your friends laugh, your pranks can sometimes go a little too far.

MOSTLY B's: BEING A LITTLE NEEDY

Of course you're attached to your friends, but it's good to know when they might need a little space!

MOSTLY C's: BEING TOO HONEST

It doesn't matter if you're snapping back with a witty comeback, speaking your mind can have unintended consequences.

MOSTLY D's: GETTING CAUGHT BORROWING SOMETHING WITHOUT PERMISSION

Friends share all the time, but it's important to ask before taking something that isn't yours!

Uh-oh! Imagine that you left an embarrassing voice mail for your friend! What did you say? Write about it below!

....

....

....

....

....

....

....

....

....

....

....

....

....

....

WOULD YOU RATHER

WOULD YOU RATHER . . .

Write a book of original songs

OR

write your own advice book?

Be possessed by a ghost

OR

Meet a cat possessed by a ghost?

Be able to read people's minds

OR

be able to move objects with your mind?

Change your last name

OR

change your entire name?

PHOEBE EDITION

Learn to play guitar with chords

OR

Make up your own name for them?

Have a big, over-the-top wedding

OR

have a small intimate ceremony in the snow?

Beat a video game

OR

beat an incessant beeping fire alarm?

Name a baby Phoebe

OR

name a baby Phoebo?

Dress up as a superhero

OR

dress up as half a Santa?

Pretend to be a doctor

OR

pretend to be an agent?

Can you figure out which *Friends* character said each line?

1.
"We were on a break!"
A. Rachel
B. Ross
C. Gunther
D. Chandler

2.
"How you doin'?"
A. Chandler
B. Ross
C. Phoebe
D. Joey

3.
"Pants: Like shorts, but longer."
A. Ross
B. Joey
C. Phoebe
D. Chandler

4.
"I've got this uncontrollable need to please people."
A. Chandler
B. Ross
C. Monica
D. Phoebe

5. "It's like all of my life everyone has always told me, 'You're a shoe!'"

A. Rachel
B. Joey
C. Phoebe
D. Monica

6. "See? He's her lobster!"

A. Joey
B. Ross
C. Monica
D. Phoebe

7. Who said the very last line in the series?

A. Ross
B. Rachel
C. Chandler
D. Monica

BONUS!

What was the last line?

....

WHAT WOULD YOU DO?

The group gets into a lot of crazy scenarios during the show. What would you do in these situations?

You are stuck in the dark during a citywide blackout:

....

....

....

You are late for a party, but your friends aren't ready to go:

....

....

....

Your friend gets stung by a jellyfish:

....

....

....

You called dibs on a chair, but
then someone stole your spot:

....

....

....

Your crush tells you they like you:

....

....

....

You find out your grandmother's homemade cookie
recipe is actually printed on the back of a bag of
chocolate chips:

....

....

....

Your friend asks you to help them pick out an outfit:

....

....

....

WOULD YOU RATHER

WOULD YOU RATHER . . .

Use a thesaurus every time you spoke

OR

constantly call everything a "moo point"?

Eat a meaty trifle

OR

eat an entire turkey in one sitting?

Hide a scary book in the freezer

OR

finish the book even if it gives you nightmares?

Use air quotes incorrectly

OR

make up a confusing way to remember the days of the week?

JOEY EDITION

Accidentally poke yourself in the eye

OR

have a hernia?

Completely miss the ball on a game show

OR

trick your friend into buying you a new fridge?

Be omnipotent for a day

OR

be omnipotent forever?

Star on a soap opera

OR

star in a Japanese commercial?

Have a neighbor that sings every morning

OR

sings every night?

Pretend to own a fancy car

OR

pretend to be a doctor?

As we see in the show, there are countless jobs to choose from, including professor, actor, and personal shopper!

What job would *you* choose if you got to work in New York City? Write down your answers on these pages, and imagine what your life would be like!

The job I would like is:

....

This job would require a lot of lessons I learned in these classes:

....

....

I would like this job because:

....

....

In this job, I would get to do things like:

....

....

....

The best part of this job would be:

....

....

....

....

....

....

The worst part of this job would be:

....

....

....

....

....

....

....

Joey gets to be on an awesome game show, but he gets a little confused with the rules!

If you were on the game show, what clues would you give your partner to guess each secret word?

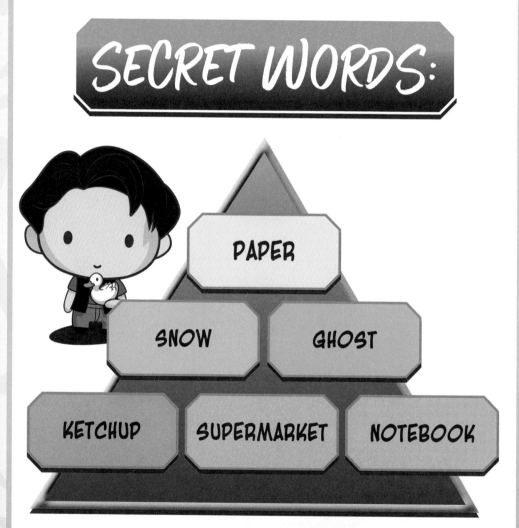

SECRET WORDS:

PAPER

SNOW

GHOST

KETCHUP

SUPERMARKET

NOTEBOOK

These are the clues I would give to guess each secret word from the previous page:

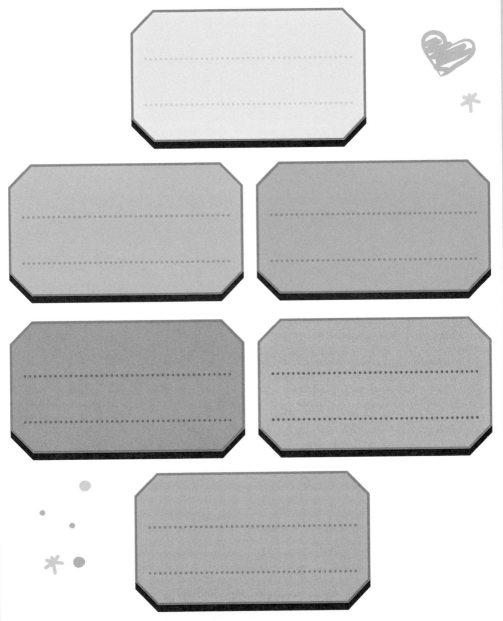

Now that you planned out your clues, see if you can get a friend to guess the secret word!

From London to Las Vegas, the six friends go on a lot of amazing adventures with one another! Imagine you were traveling with them and check off your choices for all the questions below to show how you'd spend the journey.

I would chose my seat on the plane:

○ BY THE AISLE   ○ IN THE MIDDLE   ○ BY THE WINDOW

I would sit:

○ WITH THE GIRLS   ○ WITH THE GUYS
○ WITH STRANGERS   ○ ALONE

I would spend the flight:

○ SLEEPING   ○ READING
○ TALKING WITH FRIENDS   ○ WATCHING MOVIES

I would get these snacks from the flight attendant:

○ POTATO CHIPS ○ SODA ○ CRACKERS
○ NOTHING—I BROUGHT MY OWN

I would change into my vacation clothes:

○ RIGHT AWAY ○ HALFWAY THROUGH THE JOURNEY
○ RIGHT BEFORE WE LANDED

WOULD YOU RATHER

WOULD YOU RATHER . . .

Use hypnosis to quit
a bad habit

OR

Make jokes
when you're
uncomfortable?

Hang out in a
steam room

OR

take a luxurious
bubble bath?

Play some racquetball
with Monica's dad

OR

do a workout with
Monica?

Stay in a job you hate
for money

OR

get hired for your
dream job with little
pay?

94

CHANDLER EDITION

Be the funny friend

OR

be the serious friend?

Wear blue lipstick

OR

wear a bunny costume?

Let your roommate do some home improvements

OR

have your neighbors wake you up with loud knocking?

Respond to everything sarcastically

OR

be the one your friends go to for advice?

Adopt a chicken

OR

adopt a duck?

Draw some travel stickers on the suitcase below.

What would you need for a trip to Barbados? Use the lines below to plan your packing list—and don't forget the sunscreen!

PACKING LIST:

....

....

....

....

....

....

....

....

Ross is a paleontologist, but he becomes a professor because he knows a lot about dinosaurs.

What's something you know a lot about that you could teach a class on? Is it your favorite sport or book series? Or your best subject at school? What sort of things would you teach your friends about this topic? Use this space to write about it.

....

....

....

....

....

....

....

....

....

WOULD YOU RATHER

WOULD YOU RATHER . . .

Have to skate around
in roller skates
all day

OR

walk around with an
eye patch?

Try on wedding
dresses with your
friends

OR

pretend to catch a
wedding bouquet?

Get stung by a
jellyfish

OR

come home to a
pigeon flying around
your apartment?

Win at foosball

OR

win at touch
football?

MONICA EDITION

Have a clean apartment but have one messy closet

OR

have a messy apartment with an organized closet?

Work at a tourist diner

OR

work at a fancy restaurant?

Do an embarrassing dance routine on national TV

OR

sing an embarrassing song during karaoke?

Dance with a turkey on your head

OR

walk around with WILDLY frizzy hair?

Phoebe can wear some fun outfits! Using the images below, color two different outfits for her to wear.

Chandler and Joey win season tickets to go see their favorite team. Imagine you're playing for your favorite sports team. Then write your answers below!

My favorite sport is:

....

I like to root for this team:

....

My favorite part of the game is:

....

My team player number would be:

....

Before the game, I like to eat:

....

....

....

....

....

Draw yourself playing with the team below!

What are the absolute funniest moments/lines in the show *Friends*? Fill out this bracket with the letters beside each phrase to find out!

A. How you doin'?!

B. We were on a break!

C. It's a trifle!

D. A moo point

E. Could I be any more . . . ?

F. PIVOT!

G. Oh. My. God.

H. Unagi

WINNER!

I. They know we know!

J. 15 Yemen Road, Yemen

K. He's her lobster!

L. Baby got back

M. What are they feeding you?

N. I, Ross, take thee Rachel

O. P as in Phoebe

P. I've got to get off this plane

Think about the friends in *your* life. Now write in who you think best applies to each category!

The person I can count on for anything is:

....

When I'm feeling down, this person can always cheer me up:

....

I would always stick up for:

....

The person who best takes care of me is:

....

If I had a million tacos, I'd share them with:

....

I look up to:

....

Someone who looks up to me is:

....

CONNECT THE DOTS!

Help Joey find his hand twin by connecting the dots!

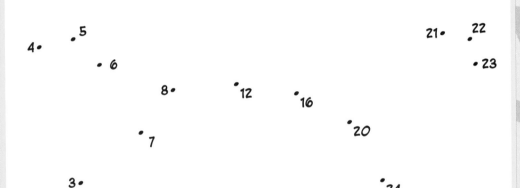

Imagine you're a scriptwriter on Joey's soap opera! You get to decide what happens next to Dr. Drake Ramoray. In the following pages, write a script for Dr. Drake Ramoray. Is he about to be the first doctor in space? Does he find true love? Will he meet his untimely end? It's your script, so you get to decide!

Pretend you're playing a trivia game about all your friends. Write some fun facts about them below!

That's it—you've made it! You must be one of the greatest friends out there, just like Ross, Rachel, Monica, Joey, Chandler, and Phoebe. Sign your name here and be on your way . . . you're a true master of the TV show *Friends*!

CERTIFICATE OF
FRIENDSHIP

F·R·I·E·N·D·S
THE TELEVISION SERIES

CENTRAL PERK